"What am I?" asked Butterfly

irst published in 2008 by © Rockpool Children's Books Ltd.

his edition published in 2018 by Rockpool Children's Books Ltd.
 association with Albury Books.
lbury Court, Albury, Thame, OX9 2LP, United Kingdom

 CIP catalogue record of this book is available from the British Library.

rinted in China

SBN 978-1-906081-24-9 (Paperback)

In the dark
green tropical
rainforest,
something stirred!

Not the
monkey
swinging
through
the trees . . .

. . . or the large,
hairy **spider**
spinning her web.

Not the **parrot**
screeching . . .
. . . or the
snake slithering

Under a large,
green leaf,
something
twitched and
twirled.

It was a tiny,
yellow **cocoon**.

It wriggled
and whirled,
and then out
popped . . .

. . . Butterfly!

But no one had told
him that he was a **butterfly**.
He felt very confused.

He had gone to bed as
a **caterpillar** . . .

. . . and woken up
with wings on his
back . . .

. . . big, bulgy
eyes . . .
. . . and
a curly,
twirly nose!

"Excuse me,
what am I?"
asked **Butterfly**.

"You don't have as
many legs as me,
so you can't be
a **millipede**!"

"Excuse me,
what am I?"
asked **Butterfly**.

"Lunch?" thought the **frog**.
But he said, "You have
big, bulgy eyes, but your skin
isn't damp and shiny,
so you can't be a **frog**!"

"Excuse me,
what am I?"
asked **Butterfly**.

"You have lovely wings,"
said the **hornbill**.
"But you don't have any feathers,
so you can't be a **hornbill**!"

"Excuse me,
what am I?"
asked **Butterfly**.

"Your nose
curls like mine,"
said the **elephant**.
"But you are very
small, so you
can't be an
elephant!"

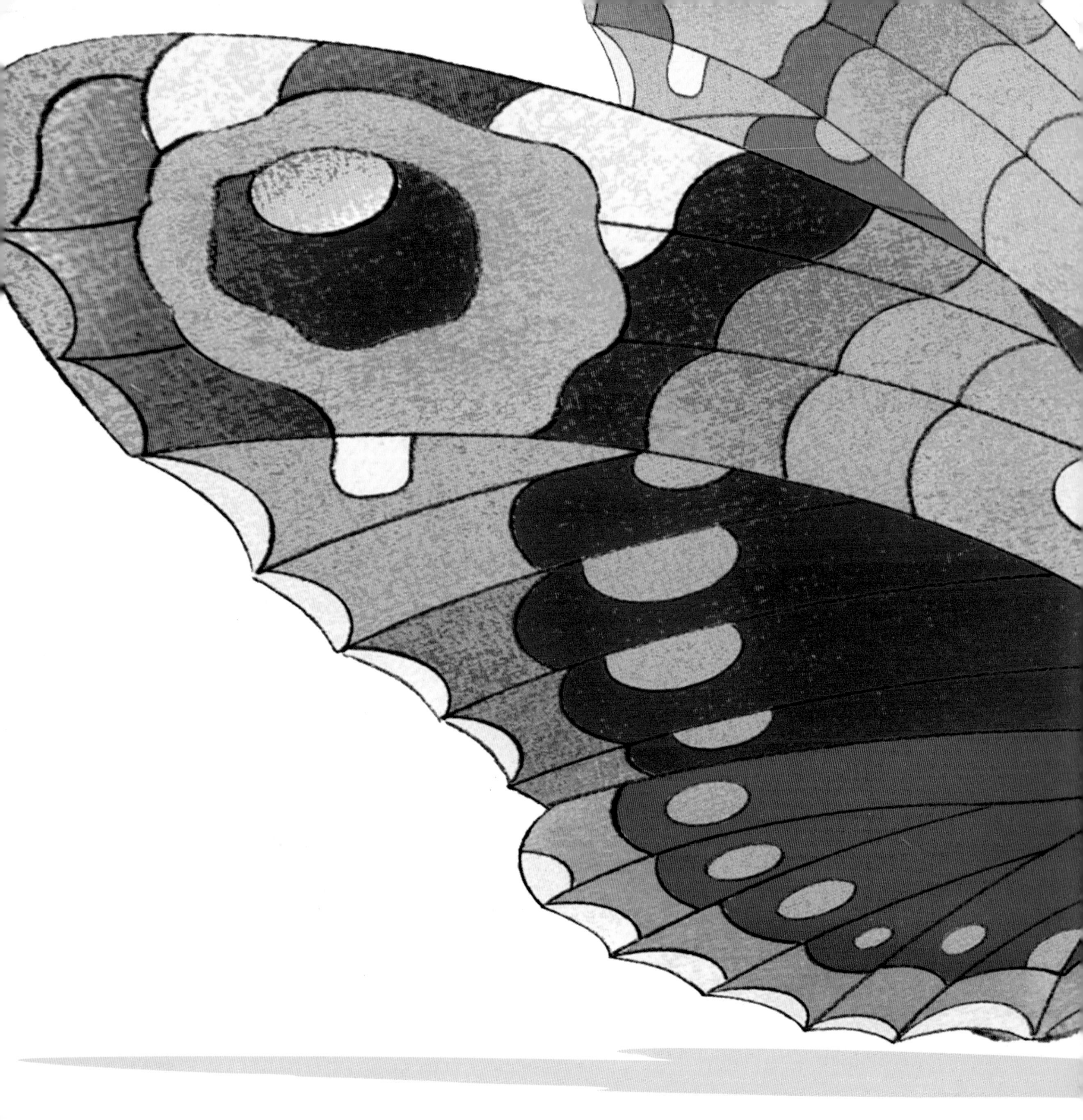

He felt very sad.
He wasn't a **millipede**
or a **frog**. He wasn't a
hornbill or an **elephant**.

"Oh, what am I?"

"I think you will find,"
said a voice,
"that you are one of us.
You are an utterly,
fluttery . . .

. . . butterfly!